My Archipelago

part pump
part chalk

Kathryn Rantala

My Archipelago by Kathryn Rantala

Copyright © 2024 by Kathryn Rantala

Cover design, cover preparation, artwork
& interior layout
by harry k stammer

ISBN: 979-8-9898666-7-0
Printed in U.S.A.

Sandy Press
Queensland, Australia
&
California, USA

https://sandy-press.com
sandypress2021@gmail.com

for helmi

Contents

Channel Islands

Coordinates

Variance of Lift

"The Roar Of The Sea And The
Plangent Cries Of Whimbrels"

The Common Air
Its Counterpoint

Channel Islands

The near, the clear, and vaunts the clearest bloom . . .

—Wallace Stevens,
"To the One of Fictive Muse"

Wandering Aengus

Hazel burst brilliantine

moons woodsfuls
the outside others
son the sun

the linnet-limbed
at deep dappled core
could not stay in

      *

green-gray waves above the spiny urchin

all the little
all the little

arc deliberates the damp dim hair

      *

host aloft
party done
lamped cats put out

brick stair hovers
wafer of the sleeping air

Haydn's Evening Letters

Ribboned floret glories of the spring tubers
Papa at the *escritoire*
registration of the strings
an air up

and in a bright red book
and in the oratorio

And Etc.

Winged Mercury
entering the felt wood
of fettered house

illumined souvenir

the wall-hung portrait of express
air wired to it
at its back

Drought Of The Land

Concentric knees
rolls of water in
the cupped canopies
the palmed palms
the rise of the meandering distance

long draft of the camel

*

in the chaparral
a bleached altitude

and in the cranial lobelia
an inexact
reaction

salts from pinched digits
lace the spiders
of periphery

*

sway animals peak
to drink slowly

met
mete
the various variety

the lily this and
that

He

Rode in road out
wholly rood
by root
brood

burdensome
then
some

gone some
gone
for good
good

Birds In The Finest Houses

Things alike a hinge
before or after
one or other
over meadow
carpet
sweep a strange stained memory

in the attic
in the loft
especially

Remodeling

A stand of trees
a walk
fear of harvest in the stalks

seas to lift you up
or drown

grass to flatten
sandy mound

Something Like Baseball

Fluttering dust pivots
the cut
blight borers
sliced light

the charming gamete
tops securely
tangling in the cool silks

Margharetta At The Still

First cold press
the dew
doe
sing of veil
in the travertine

*

dawn
the dimple sloe

wimpling wet electrics
rush the down drone
done
domine
domine

drip coil gullet of the long way

The Land of Chinoiserie

Alive the succulent crustacean

red box
fisted bee

the hinge of paper
nothing to the steep light

The Dinner Party

Sag-lipped candles
basking
flasks
the floor on fire

goodbye to the other
goodbye to the other

sill of the evening

      *

guests let out

the yard in eely sweat
pings with moons

I serpentine
a scuffed ball

Pride And The Careful

Between evening
and *The Song of Bernadette*
a bedroom urn
doubled by the glass
looked in
from off the roof

wet and
righteous as a lord

The Two-Railed Train

Not nod nor shuffle
glass
nor ruffled doubling door
nor

ask instead
the louvered bird

Fall

A bundled stationary place

leapers leap
and in the diacritical
bashed
and unabashed
unafraid

not ecstasy of stag
this
against the moon

The Service

Gloved face
for no kisses

ledges
pots
wind

The Mango Pots Of Veuve Rantala

The spider has for circuit
shortened
crushed consideration

flushed trees
webbed mangoes

pots abide abodes of hiss
strange champagnes
drown the lucky snake
in his

every day a beading rain

Parade II

Or winter
or the hardly out
outside processions
of the equinoxes

COORDINATES

When music is far enough away . . .
objects are as still as lavender

—Frank O'Hara,
"A Quiet Poem"

64.4651° N, 24.2625° E

it was winter and winter and winter
one sleeping one dreaming
summer and so on
sun and moon
tern and feather
and so on

[Pyhäjoki, Finland]

47.6580° N, 117.4235° W

boat
rounds
a lark to west

so another want of it
and nest

downy bosom
gathered
out
and out

my best

[Astoria, Oregon]

46.1693° N, 123.3801° W

parts of land
variably close to water

some wet
some the waited for

nothing changes this
nothing changes

[Puget Island, Washington]

48.4201° N, 122.3375° W

turned tables
turned legs
an oval pulls broadwater

a hesitant narrows the icy tern
under
under
the down stone duck

[Mount Vernon, Washington]

48.7767° N, 121.8144° W

lungs tighten
air stops
digits
curl their vegetative ends

scrape of granite
skins
chink

      *

nor rise
nor billowed verity
nor wounded pump
lightly
in the icy
altitudes

[Mount Baker, Washington]

47.4018° N, 122.3243° W

a waxing gibbous
patent null
dims
rises
dims
rises

[Des Moines, Washington]

47.8107° N, 122.3774° W

sun as far
as out
as fat

mind's bees blowing through the intersections

buds one
or one or
more than
and

[Edmonds, Washington]

45.5152° N, 122.6784° W

cold in your displeasure
in the whites
that end
white arms

morsels
bits
no spoon gets under
lifts

[Portland, Oregon]

45.4562° N, 123.8440° W

blossoming night pocket
lengthening light
eventually refusing a close time

fields of leaf-bough
the brittle
the elastics
visible
wide

[Tillamook, Oregon]

47.6580° N, 117.4235°W

spilled basket
weather dropped by talons

sun moon
fluted things
ache the more for

nothing yawps the lesser mumbles
of sequestery

[Spokane, Washington]

40.9168° N, 74.1718° W

this in so variable crow
notices a feather
loose

plucks and
drops
shined obsidian

[Paterson, New Jersey]

55.6761° N, 12.5683° E

the pine
the spiny arch
point to time had
in the gauzy gardens

proximal

were this the
this
the only

[Copenhagen, Denmark]

52.3676° N, 4.9041° E

edged cheeses
asked to stand

disconnective tissues
go in ways
the elephantiasis
holds Edvard

round round
the cockling labyrinths
the merciful canal

[Amsterdam, Netherlands]

50.1109° N, 8.6821° E

the Beloveds
in display
in long looking low museum light

betrothed before the fire
betrothed after

[Frankfurt, Germany]

2.1920° N, 13.7289° E

bouldered god
shouldered ease
for ease
a woolly this
a cloven that
his (somewhere
lost)
antediluvian sheep

[Abruzzo, Italy]

41.7498° N, 12.6485° E

morning evening blue orange Tuscany
Bologna
gold and red
Venezia enmasked

floods and
south the Minotaur
and
no end to it

[Gandolfo, Italy]

12.0464° S, 77.0428° W

purples
greens
mustards
lithe
among the lupines

Vallejo
pre
the road
the rain
post Paris
Spain

as century has a face
human
shard
and brace

[Lima, Peru]

35.8617° N, 104.1954° E

coal clarifies
the outline
fossil hand
both north
and sleep

spirals
measure me
for shrinkage

[Kunming, China]

51.2787° N, 0.5217° E

the lion
bat
the sooty mangabey
or yet the fortunes of a spent bee
do not think the thing you see

[Kent, England]

The Variance Of Lift

And the world goes by,
all the worlds, each more beautiful than the last . . .

—Louise Glück, "Poem" from
Winter Recipes from the Collective

And At The Feet Of June

Andalusian banns
the standing owls
the cowls
the basketries of hands

luminous green
the beautiful Lorca

tact
in its graceful skins
tact
in its graceful skins

A Leap Observed

As moon flashed the branch mire bewindowed

it was
as they say
the night spindle

rub orb teeth glass
ticklishly enmeshed

Big Little

Prickled beach
the smell
the tide
foot all splay
shell
all ride

fathomed
idled
pulled aside

I Did Not Know You Were Coming

My hand a plate
a cup
thumbs
fingers
eye a fish
idling with the eels
my mouth a line

Achene

Silk would warm apparent vessel
iridic moon would splay
its sheer elongate thirst

still vertical from God
she all at once
subtracts

that directly over
keeps her
shadow

In South

Groaty bugs and
not all compline music

in last canon hours
sweet smells
as under
God's complicated chin

Little Big

And one of these
should be about
the tendril
short of stabling
The House of Wisteria
by a tall inch

A Branched Bird Tilts

Hard to look square at me
in thicket

I bolt home green
the red
unraveling

the bushy potato plant sees me

The Invariorum

An arrow through the Earth
predicts a horse
its brightened neck
circling the Palace
of Versailles

unleathered
on the slippy glacial till
anvil hooves
roll redacted fossils
leaves

beware
time's lovelies
the king aloft
the whitened eyes
an old day starts

Letting Lie

And if one desires
patient
with broadleaf umbers of restraint
so one should not wish
less for less
as tadpoles lie and lie again
between the great ledges

above the sought and padded place
leapers lie the longer
bashed and unabashed
and unafraid
then then the night side of maundering
lifts sequence for edge

so
sleep sleep
letting lie who may
as temporary sounding sounds a bay
and nothing
in particular
particularly dawns

Coming Back

If in April
wan and weal
if a dog
a spiny eel
if the existential mouse

if August or the trembling bale
if start or wail
in a long or smaller place
if lidded heart or boulder face

if sun
with tautened line and creel
if quickening
a shiny reel

Epistemology: Three French Thens

Alors
The pandering nature of sauce

Puis
Above the flower urn
we darken
heave and drop

sprite right
sprite left
peer into
a courage of contained bloom

Ensuite
He may visit in the ballroom

wind
as fast as
still not changing him

very
very
there

As If They Were A Basket

As I am
as were a born thing
as near the mouse as wing
in latitudes that thin the bones

as snowy owl or bee
in their geometry
as camel bison fish
antelope and mole
thirsty as a root
safe as thistle
and consistent with a long light
as carnivore or prey
in cascading blithe array

as they
as any as I or
as a cow beneath a tree
as ashes
bear the ash
in their constituency
as if they were a basket

Stride Piano

Balancing on nails
note and chord
note and chord

hearing
as in constellation

sun
as in the present
sequent

light and next
light and next

at the window
birds
to bat

the break
of under-
taking

sorry

as in misplacement

sorrow
(as in
constellation)

the nonce
a wove ruin

Do Not Touch

West of certainty
through trades
to light
and wind
under/on as chevron
lap
not cast
nor moored
least assured

A Land Of Papyrus

Chaos
(more the south)
in fields of reeds
and easements
aisles
shafts
pass to almost passing
passed

you are nowhere in it now

a copy of
a string of beads

"The Roar Of The Sea And The Plangent Cries Of Whimbrels"

words attributed to Gudrid the Far Traveler

1

On crumbling earth-edge
the urge to curl
from inside bending
impulse shell-advancing

cones dragged water stones
down in the roar
behind the ammonites

looked at from another long time
only farther
and from straightened out

2

it was a windy wide place
a curlew missing everything
in chevrons

my breath drawn out
too big
to wrap the arms around

the winded pines
the ground still standing
headings now unclear
and maybe
anyway
blown back

3

from here a froth ran toward the rocks
as if it wanted to
an eye from shore
a bird too
a beach in place of active
the still inside the heart
right as sink in muck

4

difficult in slant wind
to know a way to face
to living or to living stone

logs tossed up
the distance between points
as how it is with us
separate
but drowned among the other

or to recall specifics
the volume
less the lessened heart

5

we didn't say he was dying
we almost kept saying it

the rimmed green algae
other things
that live in things a while

an overhanging arch
the dangling turf roots
artifacts of shade
the sharp smelling surf
all unpotable

a day too wet to find
in a week of wet

sweeps of terraces
cuts
hot then cold
and instead of lying down
running from the shore
as fast as possible

6
one day at the end of the world
a raven or a tide
wandering the general west
transforming
or was it still

the sun inventing fall
on sides of leaves
I think I dropped straight down

water hit back
hard
a roll of cold
as stones roughed up against the others and

little
beyond a totem
a stack of rocks
a flat fish
to promise anyone

The Common Air
Its Counterpoint

1
The arch
the merely angel
angled toward epiphany
portentous
punctuate
and in the aftermath
elaborate

the air
the air prehensile
buffs the thin-haired women
light-struck deer the vole

eels
in their sand
divine divinity
in each other
and the many-legged
and the fish
hold
hold tentacular

hosta God is leaf
succulent
in water it is sure of

love songs of the sanguine
in the draw
the rock

2
fire out
pendants
lost in clerestory
the small in antiphonic dark

untitled urban trail
unsupporting rail
thrush V. nest

worthies press advantage
add/subtract the magpie
the metronomic tail
the vest

frosted everything
the heart
raptor shrew
the unaware
assembling
pleased as music
in the ammonite's
tympanic folds

mergings merged
the heart diaphanous
its folds
prolonged as difficult

3
of caverns
cranium is first

viscera and all
the ache of roots
primarily
exhaling

what in host has stilled
what cannot be reduced
perhaps congruent
as arrayed

mantis
in the mystery of objects
all knees and longing
in the chapel of the still
its ligatures of praise

wake us
come and wake us closed and closed
wake and wake and
like a hungry fish wake us
furtive in the corals

eclipse will fit itself
its filigrees of doubt
were we very tired
were we very merry
were we given least instruction
the intricately sad
the long-limbed
rose and idled
and in some way failed

conflation
irritation
in some way

  4
say the prudent opening of windows
made a flare
a gust
a gingered guest
decanting

dessication's apparatus
repeat
dessication's apparatus

snow against the side with light
slow
V. sub- or extra-liminal
the rise of prisms in the land

paleo buttes
part devotional
part crush
in escarpment
in the catacombs
the lofts
a slope aside redemption

andante
as to that
cantabile
warren
for the shortest sense of mortise

most in air
the wheels mesh most freely
accordions of marsh
the preen
and in the liveries
the languorous
the sift of aeries
silts
dropped down ground

chill today
tomorrow boiling down a hole

5

saddest of the scrape
the footholds
rushes reeds
the brandished and below
the segmented
immaculately veined
and blind as casings

the fields of pistil stamen
transept nave
and in the aisle
a musculo-membranous tube

6

oleander in the sacristy
drifting intra
intermittence

in a movie we went into a house

effigies of fish
the feint
the faintly fathomed

the house did nothing
the trees outside did nothing

measuring has weight
irises water

diluvian
alluvial
decidedly

the vice of simple things

mortal storms for mangroves
the foyer
abattoir
mandrake
mephistoph

some disinclination some holiness

and Lazarine

as calendar
as weather
as no day whatsoever

it was hot where we were

tired tried
jittered in the aspens
the rub
the boundaries of stag
continuity
the molt

the house did not care

submersions
or the offerings

part chalk
part pump

the trees did not care

nobis
pro
if pre-iterative greens commingle

anomic
anomie
anemones of needles

bless
as past a shoulder bless
the plumbed
the strange
the temporary

it was lovely

Acknowledgments

The author wishes to thank Marc Kipniss and Rebecca Loudon for their early support of this work, as well as the editors of these journals where these poems first appeared:

3rd bed, Alba, Ampersand, Blue Fifth Review, elimae, fail-better, Fiera Lingue, Ice River, Locus Points, Magazine of Speculative Poetry, New Orleans Review, Oyster Boy Review, Poems Niederngasse, Riven, Siren, Sleeping Fish, Three Candles, Utriculi.

About the Author

Kathryn Rantala lives in Edmonds, Washington, and is the author of *A Little Family, The Finnish Orchestra, 3 Letters & Julius* and other works of poetry and short fiction. Her collaboration with Camano Island artist Jack Gunter on "The Jack Gunter Collection," a three-volume set of poetry and art, is available at ravennapess.com beginning October, 2024. Kathryn is also a visual artist, creating stills, portraits, and assemblages from found objects. She has exhibited regionally and occasionally incorporates her art into her writing. Samples of her work may be found on her website at kathrynrantala.com.